Postman Pat
and the Big Balloons

EGMONT

It was a sunny morning in Greendale. Postman Pat had a special delivery to collect from Pencaster Mail Centre.

When he arrived, Ben, the general manager, was waiting next to a parcel tied to a forklift truck.

"We don't need the truck for this one, it's small enough to carry," Pat said, and he began to untie the parcel.

"I wouldn't do that if I were you . . ." Ben began.

But he was too late! The parcel floated up into the air!

"I don't know what's in that box," said Ben, "but it has to be delivered to Reverend Timms at the Town Hall."

Pat climbed up on to the balcony and tried to grab the floating box. But it was just out of reach.

Then Jess suddenly leaped off the balcony and landed right on top of it! The parcel came down.

"Well done, Jess!" cried Pat. "Let's get it into the van."

Before they set off, Ben had another job for Pat.

"Can you drop a parcel at Ted's Garage on your way?" asked Ben. "It's for his latest invention."

"No problem!" said Pat, and he set off with his deliveries.

A few minutes later, Pat pulled up at Ted's Garage.

"I've got a special delivery for you, Ted!" he smiled.

Ted opened the parcel and pulled out a can of oil.

"Great! It's for my new invention," said Ted, picking up a long silver stick. "'The Ted Glenn Automatic Extendable Picker-up Device'!"

Ted pressed a button and the stick suddenly grew much longer and shot toward Jess!

"Watch out!" Pat chuckled, as Jess dived out of the way.

"So, what else have you got today?" Ted asked, peeping inside Pat's van.

He let out a loud gasp when he saw the floating box! He reached in and poked it, making the box wobble.

"Careful, Ted!" Pat cried. But it was too late. The box bobbed towards Ted and flew out of the back of the van!

Ted made a lunge for the box but he only managed to grab the string that was tied around it. Then the string came undone and the box flew open!

A big bunch of helium balloons floated out of the box and up into the Greendale sky!

"Quickly! We've got to catch them before they disappear!" gasped Pat. "Ted, we'll need your new invention and a ladder. Follow those balloons!"

Pat and Jess jumped in the van and drove after the runaway balloons. Ted wasn't far behind in his truck.

The balloons drifted into a nearby tree. Pat and Ted pulled over and went to have a look.

Ted tried to grab the balloons with his invention, but it wasn't quite long enough. The balloons were still stuck up in the branches of the tree.

"Let's use the ladder," Pat suggested. "That should do it."

Pat was just balancing the ladder up against the tree when PC Selby appeared.

"What's going on here then?" he boomed.

Pat quickly told PC Selby all about the runaway balloons.

"This is a job for an officer of the law," replied PC Selby, and he began to climb up the ladder himself! When he reached the top, he untied one of the balloons.

"That's it, PC Selby!" shouted Pat, from down below.

But when he went to untie another balloon, he didn't have a free hand. The ladder wobbled and PC Selby started to get worried.

"I don't know what to do, Pat!" PC Selby shouted down. "I can't free the other balloons without letting this one go!"

"Tie the balloon on to one of the buttons on your jacket!" Pat called. "Then your hands will be free to get the others!"

So PC Selby tied the balloon string on to a button. Soon enough, he had tied all of the balloons on to his jacket.

Then, as he started to climb back down, he slipped. But instead of falling, PC Selby floated up to the sky!

Meanwhile, over at the Town Hall, the residents of Greendale were gathering for a celebration. Reverend Timms had organised a Town Hall re-opening party.

"Pat should be here with my delivery by now!" Reverend Timms exclaimed.

Then Meera glanced up to the sky and gasped. Everybody else looked up too, and they saw the bunch of balloons floating past, with PC Selby dangling beneath them!

"That's my special delivery!" cried Reverend Timms.

Back at Pencaster Street, Pat was wasting no time. PC Selby was floating towards the Harbour so he had to be quick!

"Ted, you wait in your boat at the Harbour," Pat began. "I'm going to get the helicopter!"

When Pat and Jess arrived at the Mail Centre, Ben was on hand to help.

Moments later, the helicopter was ready. Pat pulled on his helmet, and the helicopter whirred into action!

PC Selby was admiring the view. "Ah, maybe this isn't so bad," he sighed, as he looked down at the village below.

But then he caught sight of the lake.

"Oh dear!" he cried. "I'm going out over the water! Help!"

Ted was ready and waiting in his boat.

"Stay calm, Arthur!" he called. "Pat is on his way!"

At the Town Hall, the children from Greendale School had arrived. Pat's son, Julian, was among them, watching the action on the lake.

Suddenly, the crowd heard a loud whirring noise in the sky as Pat flew past in the helicopter!

"That's my dad!" cried Julian. "He'll save PC Selby!"

Pat hovered the helicopter above PC Selby. But the wind from the helicopter's rotor blades kept pushing the policeman away from him.

"I'm going to try something else!" Pat called out.

Pat made the helicopter fly lower and used the wind from the rotor blades to push PC Selby down. Soon, he was floating just above Ted's boat.

"Can you grab hold of the mast?" Pat cried.

"I'll try, Pat!" said PC Selby, but he couldn't quite reach it.

Suddenly, there was a loud BANG as one of the balloons burst! The crowd gasped as poor PC Selby plunged towards the water.

"**N**ow, grab the mast!" Pat shouted quickly.

PC Selby was bouncing around but he finally managed to get hold of the mast. Then he climbed down on to the boat.

A huge cheer erupted from the crowd! But their relief soon turned to concern when PC Selby's jacket slipped off and whooshed up into the sky!

Pat grabbed Ted's invention. He reached out of the helicopter and caught the jacket and balloons.

The crowd cheered again. Pat had saved the day!

Pat landed the helicopter in front of the Town Hall. One by one, he handed out the balloons to the children. But when he got to Meera he was one balloon short.

"You can share mine, Meera," Julian offered, kindly. Meera beamed as Julian gave her the balloon to hold.

"Well done, Pat!" Reverend Timms said, happily. "You saved PC Selby and got the balloons here on time."

"Special Delivery Service: mission accomplished!" said Pat.

EGMONT

We bring stories to life

First published in Great Britain 2009 by Egmont UK Limited
239 Kensington High Street, London W8 6SA
Postman Pat ® © 2009 Woodland Animations Ltd.,
a division of Entertainments Rights PLC.
Licensed by Entertainment Rights Distribution Limited.
Original writer John Cunliffe. From the original television design by Ivor Wood.
Royal Mail and Post Office imagery is used by kind permission of Royal Mail Group plc.

ISBN 978 1 4052 4531 9
1 3 5 7 9 10 8 6 4 2
Printed in Italy